I0761005

sapphire

K. Mostafa

Published by Shush Books
Shush Books is a division of Shaherazad Shelves
shaherazadshelves.com

Our books may be purchased in bulk for promotional, educational, or business use. Please contact your local bookseller or Shaherazad Shelves or by email at publishing@shaherazadshelves.com
First edition, 2025
Cover design by Samiha Hoque
ISBN 978-1-960323-32-3 (hardcover)

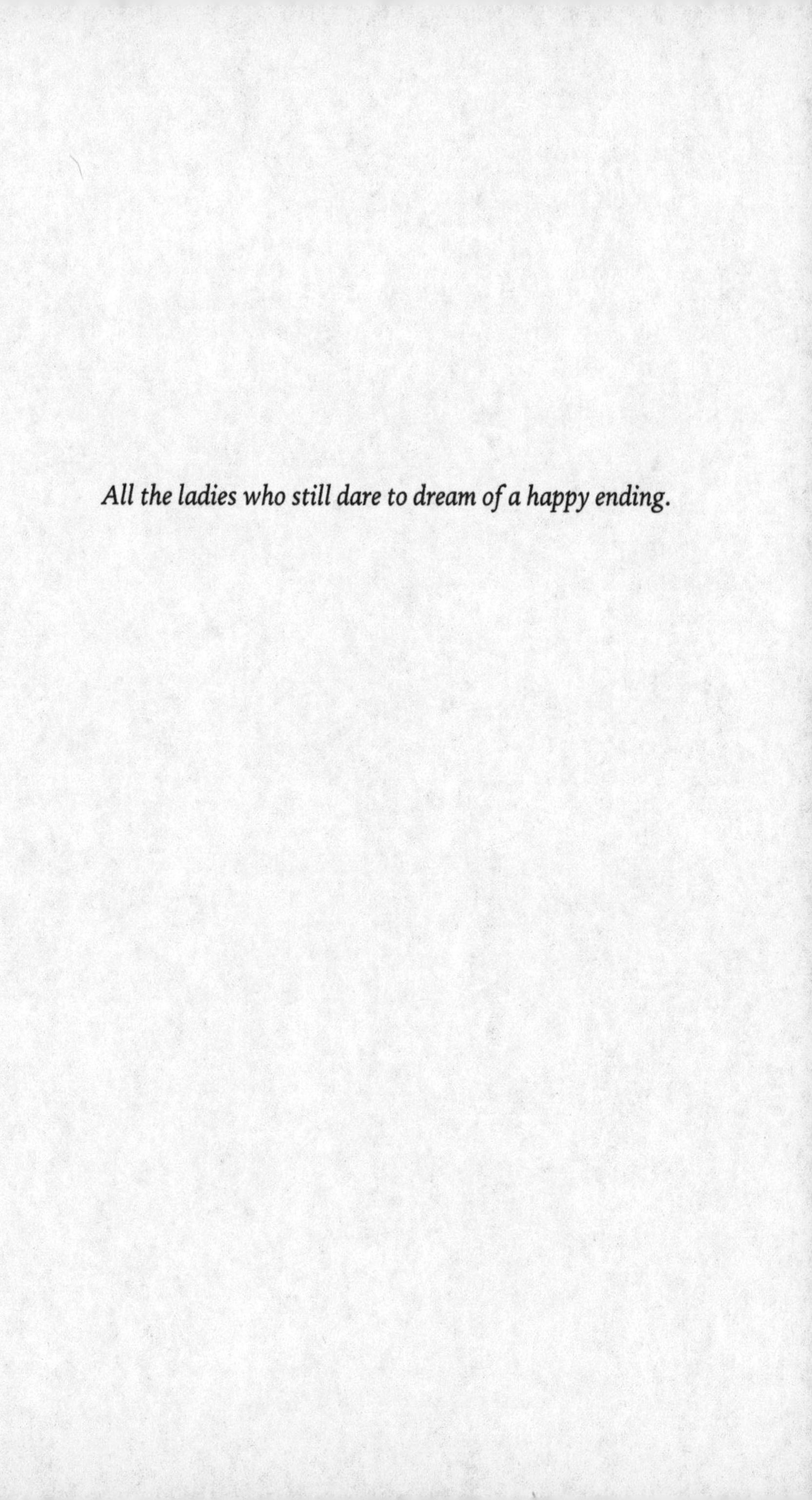

All the ladies who still dare to dream of a happy ending.

one
blue

I MET HIM AT A FAIR.

The unbearable heat was battering down on my shoulders. People were flooding through the gates in clusters. In every direction my eyes went, there were bodies flocking together, grinding and colliding with one another. I could feel my clothes clinging to my back due to the humidity, and my hair sticking to the sides of my face and neck. I stood in a comparatively quiet corner, my eyes running over the crowd of faces walking by, desperately hoping to catch a glimpse of the group of sisters I had been estranged from.

Three men were lazily pacing near me, their eyes sizing me up and down. The desperate glint in their gazes made me uncomfortably self-aware of my body. I flitted my eyes away from them and kept them locked in a different direction as if I was blissfully unaware of their dirty looks, but my hands discreetly dragged my chiffon scarf over my chest.

The men pointed out a spot on my arm to each other and let out loud, boisterous laughs. I couldn't hold my curiosity, so I looked down my shoulder.

There was a gaping split in my sleeve, exposing the skin under it. I wasn't sure how it happened, but the frayed threads indicated that it was the work of something sharp. My face flushed with embarrassment. Though I was fully clothed, the small piece of bare flesh suddenly made me feel naked in those men's eyes. The scarf loosely wrapped over my shoulders was too sheer to cover the hole, and I was afraid of moving it from its place in case I ended up flashing those men something else. So I hastily moved my fingers to pinch the hole shut. My eyes grew more desperate as I searched for my sisters.

That's when he came to me.

I don't know if it was the helpless look on my face or the malice in those men's eyes that made him want to help out—but Sharaf was the only one from the sea of people who stepped forward. He stood in front of me, blocking those men's view, and looked down at me.

His rich brown eyes locked with mine for the first time.

"Are you okay?" he asked. He was shouting over the racket around us, but there was a gentleness in his tone that caused a strange sensation in my stomach.

I first eyed him with distrust. He was tall and broad-shouldered, his facial features were very typical of Bengali men, and there was a shadow of beard on his jaw. His clothes and the way he carried himself told me he belonged to a reputable family. My mind warned me that he is a stranger, but I could already feel my heart beginning to trust him over his appearance.

I swallowed the lump in my throat before answering. "I came here with my relatives, but now I can't find them," I admitted meekly. "And my phone is dead."

He shoved a hand inside his pocket without a second thought and brought out his cell phone. "Here," he said, offering it to me. "You can use mine."

I eagerly took his phone from his palm and dialed my sister's number. I prayed under my breath as the phone rang and let out a sigh as she received it. I named a few of the stores around me to give her an estimation of my location.

I peeked at him from my peripheral vision. He was now slightly leaning towards me—decreasing the height between us—but not so much that it would make me feel uncomfortable. His eyes followed my movements.

He was scrutinizing me like those men had previously, but the difference between the nature of their gazes was like that of the sky and the ground. Those men made my skin crawl, but his look made the muscles in my stomach sensitive to the fluttering in it as if I had just jumped off a very high cliff.

I ended the conversation and hastily handed him his phone back.

"Thanks," I breathed.

His eyes darted towards the tear in my dress, making me even more self-conscious than before—if possible. I pinched my fingers harder.

He looked around, his eyes landing on a small stall with neon scarves hanging from the hooks. He walked towards it and gestured for me to follow him.

Despite my incessant protests, he picked a silk blue scarf and paid the saleswoman for it. He handed it to me.

"I don't have the money to pay you back."

"You don't need to."

"I can't accept this," I repeated, shaking my head.

"I insist."

The resolution in his eyes made me reach out for the scarf with hesitant fingers. I took it and wrapped it around my shoulders. I untucked my hair and fanned it over my back.

He was still watching me with that look in his eyes.

"I will return your money once my cousins arrive," I said.

"I won't accept it."

"Then I can't take this..." I started unraveling the scarf from around me.

"Stop, stop," he cried, raising both his hands in protest. "If you insist on paying me back, how about you give me your name?"

I stopped mid-unravel. He was staring at me wide-eyed, his expression innocent, but his lips were tugged upwards in a playful smile.

He wanted nothing, and it was everything.

I saw my cousins at a distance, walking by the stalls lining the busy pathway.

I turned to look at him, his head now turned towards them as well. His face was unreadable.

"Neela," I said under my breath.

He met my eyes again, surprise flickering in them.

I suddenly felt the urge to escape from him. My legs started moving by their own accord, and before I knew it, I was running at full speed away from him, never once looking back to see the amused look on his face.

two
honor

THE NEXT TIME I saw him was at my cousin's wedding.

I was in the middle of throwing flower petals, greeting guests, and welcoming them inside when those rich brown eyes met mine for the second time. My hand halted midair. A gasp left my lips.

Sharaf was just as surprised to see me—if the way he widened his eyes was any indication.

"Neela." His voice reached my ear, uttering my name slowly.

He wasn't allowed to stand and was ushered inside, forced to keep the flow going.

The place was crowded, filled with people donned in sequins and shiny jewelry. In the midst of it all, I kept seeing him. He was everywhere: at the stage, the dinner table, and the snacks area. I couldn't avoid him; his tall frame stood apart in the crowd, the patterns on his black sherwani slowly etching themselves into my brain.

Sharaf's brown eyes followed my every movement.

My stomach started doing that thing again. The tingles returned. I had trouble swallowing even my favorite paratha rolls.

"Who is he?" one of my cousins leaned into my ear and asked.

I couldn't speak. I only shook my head.

"Why is he staring at you?" There was displeasure in another cousin's voice. "Doesn't he know it's haram? He should be lowering his gaze."

The rights and wrongs of the situation were overlooked by the restless butterflies in my stomach.

I was called to the stage by the bride. I was fixing the pleats of my cousin's saree when the photographer wanted a picture. I sat beside the bride and smiled. A minute later, I heard my cousins giggling from below.

I looked to my right, where everyone's gazes were. The first thing I noticed was the pattern of the black sherwani. The next, my eyes found his. He had been talking to the groom on the other side of the stage, unaware of my presence. When the picture was clicked, we were both in the frame.

My heart threatened to leap out of my chest as my eyes stayed on his, even if for a moment. Sharaf's lips curled up in that playful grin again when he realized what had happened. I was taken back to the moment in the fair when he had asked for my name.

I swallowed. I was a bundle of nerves.

Just like the previous time, purely out of reflex, I briskly got up from my seat and ran away again.

I couldn't eat. I couldn't sleep. I stayed up night after night thinking of deep brown eyes and patterns on a black sherwani.

It was crazy. I didn't even know him, but I couldn't stop thinking about him. The way he said my name, the way he looked at me, and the way he sneakily smiled when he found things amusing. Just the thought of that man hollowed my stomach out and erupted tingles.

Whispers of the stolen glances and forbidden smiles reached my mother. People kept asking about how he knew me, why did he say my name, why did we take a photo together. I had never associated with a boy outside my family before. So this was strange, and it caught people's attention.

My mother started talking to my father about marriage. He wasn't pleased.

"She just graduated University, and now she's going to pursue a Master's. She's too young to get married," my father responded grumpily. Though some girls in my society failed to continue education after entering a marriage, I knew his reaction had nothing to do with it. My family was satisfied with the level of education I achieved. Neither did it have anything to do with my age. My father was upset because I was his baby. He didn't want to have to think about giving away his firstborn daughter.

"We have no choice," my mother told him. "People are talking. If we don't try to tie the knot soon, do you know what they will say?"

She had him at that. What will people say? Family's name, honor, and reputation came above all else. My father caved.

My parents reached out to his. Sharaf wasn't ready for a marriage. He had just started a job. He wasn't financially stable enough to support a family or fund a wedding, for that matter.

But he was a man of honor, and he couldn't turn his back on me.

Our families met and fixed a date. Though Sharaf wasn't in a position to finance a family, his parents were well off. They agreed to take the responsibility.

three
moonlight

IN THE MONTHS leading up to the wedding, I spoke to him on the phone a couple of times.

He was a gentleman. He was sweet. His words had the power to make me feel intoxicated.

We had two ceremonies—a reception led by a Mehndi Night.

The Mehndi Night was organized by the girls' side, only for the ladies. I was dressed in a bright orange and green lehenga, my limbs decorated with fresh flowers. The guests started arriving one by one, all dressed in bright colors and full of joy.

The evening was spent on laughter, rich food, and henna—lots and lots of it. My arms were covered with the scented, green herb paste from my fingertips to my elbow. It was tradition to write the husband's name on the bride's hands; it was an inside joke between the girls that the color of the henna determined the depth of a husband's love.

It was late when my cousins told me to go to the rooftop. I was cradling my cat, Billu, in my arms.

"Where are you taking me?" I asked, astonished as they wiped away the now-dry henna to roll down my sleeves. The scraped bits fell like rain from my arms. "We'll get in trouble if Maa catches us!"

"Just come with us!" they insisted.

The guests were still around. The spirits were still high. The rich smell of the food still wafted in the air. I had to let go of Billu. He jumped from my lap with a dissatisfied meow.

I was taken to the rooftop with my eyes tied with a piece of cloth. I was pushed into the empty terrace as I heard my cousins giggle in the distance. The blindness caused terror in my heart. I was always afraid of the dark. I struggled to take off the cloth around my eyes. When I finally managed to undo the blindfold, my heart leaped out of my chest.

Sharaf was grinning at me.

He had that same look in his eyes. That same smile. The moon was faintly smiling over our heads, too, its bluish-silver glow casting a shadow more than light.

I gasped. I looked over my shoulder. One of my cousins shouted, "Surprise!"

I turned to look at him again, a shy smile making its way to my face. This was the first time I had seen him since we got engaged. The man I was getting married to, whose name was stained on my hand.

He looked different in the shadow of the moon than he did in the light of the sun. But he was the same man, the one who was making my heart race in my chest just like he did the first time.

He was staring at my features, too, drinking them up. "You look beautiful, Neela," he whispered under the witness of the moon.

I looked down, unable to bear his gaze anymore, and the smile on my face widened beyond my control. I simply laid my palms in front of him, showing him my dried henna, now patched with green and red. But his name was still visible as prominently as his place in my heart.

I heard a voice in the distance. My blood chilled in my veins. We weren't married yet, so meeting him like this wasn't permitted. Sharaf's brows shot up in surprise.

"Oh no!" one of my cousins shrieked. "Your mother is coming."

I looked over my shoulder. He simply looked amused.

"C'mon, Neela," another cousin called. "The illegally imported man can not be seen!"

I faced him again, my eyes distressed. The intensity of his gaze was still the same.

"Go," Sharaf whispered, voice just a whisker of the wind. "I'll see you soon."

His voice raised the hair on my body. I spun on my heels, about to leave.

"Wait," he called out. "Don't forget this." He hastily handed me the piece of cloth my cousins had used to tie my eyes, which I had let slip from my hands. I looked down at it. I realized it was the same silk blue scarf he had gotten for me at the fair. A color I disliked since I was a child, but gladly accepted and embraced since it was offered by *him*.

My cousins called me. I looked over my shoulder, watching their impatient faces, and then I grabbed the scarf from his hand and ran away from him. With one last forbidden glimpse over my shoulder, I disappeared through the door frame, the trail of my skirt sliding after me.

four
sacrifice

OUR WEDDING CEREMONY took place on the morning of our reception.

It was a clear day. The sky was a bright blue. Birds chirped in the distance pleasantly. The cool breeze blowing kept the humidity at bay. It seemed like even nature was celebrating my happiness.

I was adorned in a simple blue salwar kameez, with my mother's worn-out zardouzi dupatta—the one she wore at her own wedding—draped over my head. My henna was stained a deep maroon on my hands. My heart fluttered with joy at the sight of the color, and whenever I caught his name written on my hands.

The religious event occurred in an intimate gathering. I was at my home and Sharaf at the local mosque, surrounded by close relatives, when we promised to become each other's for life.

The moment I accepted my marriage to him and signed my name, my mother's tears started flowing.

"Our daughter is no longer ours," she was weeping.

Her words gutted me. There was happiness in my heart for becoming a wife, but how could the parents who raised me cease to have rights over me in the blink of an eye?

I was barely given any time to process my feelings. The majority of my day was spent getting ready for the reception. We hired a makeup artist who would come to my house and work on my face. My attire for the occasion was a red and gold Banarasi sharee, chosen by Sharaf's family. My aunts couldn't stop gushing over how beautiful I looked in it.

I *felt* just as beautiful, my heart flooding with joy at the realization that I was finally his.

I was in the middle of getting dressed when I was called by my mother to finish packing the suitcases I would be taking to my new home with me. My makeup artist granted me a short break, and I headed toward my room. Clothes were hanging from the closet, and my belongings were spread on the floor. Twenty-five years of my life were being packed in a handful of bags. My mother and sister were trying to find a method to the madness, attempting to fit more things in the suitcases that were already overstuffed. I started organizing the bags of cat food I had purchased, knowing my fussy

Billu wouldn't survive a day without his particular kind.

I glanced at the black-and-white cat with fondness, licking its own paw in silence in his corner of my room. I found him on the side of our street when he was still a baby. The poor thing was barely surviving on the garbage casually cast aside by people. I took him in and nurtured him to full health. Now, the nawab refused to consume anything but high-class packaged food.

My mother looked at me. Her eyebrows reached her hair.

"What are you doing?" she asked.

"Packing Billu's stuff," I replied, eyes still on the work at hand.

"But he's not going with you."

My heart dropped to my stomach. I halted, mouth opening in shock. "Why not?" I asked.

She let out a sigh and pursed her lips. "Silly girl, who takes her cat to her in-laws?" She shook her head affectionately.

I was at a loss for words. I blinked at her, wondering if she was joking.

"What do you mean?" I cried with disbelief. "Billu is my baby. I can't live without him."

"It doesn't work like that, Neela. Besides, it was finalized beforehand that the cat is staying behind. Sharaf doesn't like pets."

"Finalized by whom?" My voice was starting to

strain with outrage. My eyes were starting to tear. "Why wasn't I informed? Nobody even consulted with me before making the decision."

Seeing the tears in my eyes, my Mom reached out to hold my hand, a look of deep sadness in her eyes. "The life of a wife is full of sacrifices," she said. " Consider this your first sacrifice as a wife for the sake of your husband's happiness." She let out a deep breath. "In the grand scheme of things, this will seem silly to you someday. You can't start to shed tears over such small matters." She patted my right hand.

Now, I was bawling. Tears were streaming down my face. Billu stared at me with nonchalance, not comprehending what was going on. The makeup artist started freaking out, telling me nothing was worth ruining my makeup on my wedding day.

five
duty

THE FIRST FEW weeks of my marriage seemed to fly in the blink of an eye. My days consisted of moments that filled my heart with joy, and then changes that choked me.

It felt like a dream to go to sleep every night with Sharaf's soft kisses and wake up every morning entangled in his arms. I could hear him call my name every day. I could watch him cast me that smile to my heart's full desire. His deep brown eyes could put me in a spell with one look, and the touch of his fingers was soon becoming more familiar to me than my own. There was nothing that gave me more joy in life than being addressed as his wife. I liked being his, and with each day spent with him, I could feel myself falling in love a little more.

Along with those sweet moments came adjustments. My parents raised us in a very simple household that focused on strong values. But my in-laws were more modern and extravagant. I realized soon I was expected to adapt to the culture of my new family—changing the way I spoke, dressed, and carried myself. It made a simple girl like me feel completely out of depth.

I knew my father and mother-in-law didn't yet expect their son to shoulder any finances of the household as Sharaf had just graduated University less than a year ago and only started his first job; in their eyes he was still a baby. However, he didn't participate in any other household responsibilities either. Since both my sister and I were taught to take on chores from a young age, I attempted to help around the kitchen from time to time—which I soon realized wasn't only accepted, but also expected of the daughter-in-law of the house even though no one asked me themselves. Along with that, my life also started consisting of dinner parties, meeting new family members, and fitting my old belongings in my new home. It was overwhelming to say the least.

A practice Sharaf soon introduced me to was going out on the evening before the weekends. We usually had dinner with his friends or cousins. Since it was the end of the week, Sharaf wasn't as stressed out by work, and we were promised a couple of hours of extra sleep the next morning. And at the end of those outings, he usually took me to check on my parents.

Sharaf never entered my parents' house. He always stayed in the garage, inside the car.

"You go," he always said. "I'll wait as long as needed."

"But don't you want to see my parents too?"

"Just go, Neela," he would say with exasperation, tired of answering the same question repeatedly.

I expressed my displeasure to my mother every time.

She clicked her tongue. "Don't be silly, Neela," she said. "A son-in-law can't just walk into his wife's parents house."

"But why?" I cried. "I live with his."

"It doesn't look good."

"I want to spend more time in this house with you and Baba. I still feel like a stranger in his." My voice faltered as I mentioned that. I could never stay with my parents for more than ten to fifteen minutes. Sharaf always said I could take my time, but I knew he was waiting, I knew it was hot. I couldn't leave him sitting in his car for longer than that.

"I want him to have a relationship with my family, too," I argued.

My mother got misty-eyed as she said, "A daughter's duties lie with her in-laws. A son's is not tied to his."

I shook my head. "It doesn't make sense."

"It's culture, it doesn't have to."

six
suspicion

IT WAS A WEEKEND. We were at a shopping mall.

My excited eyes ran over the multicolored clothes kept in stacks of folds, shoes of different styles, jewelry gleaming from their racks. The vendors were calling out to us from the shops, displaying their best products to attract our attention.

His sister and I were hopping from stall to stall. She clutched my right hand and dragged me to a little corner displaying reshmi churis. Her eyes gleamed at the variations of the glass bangles.

"Here, try these out," she said, holding up half a sleeve in the air. "They're blue. You know Sharaf loves blue."

My heart fell in love with the beauties at first sight. They were blue. It was his favorite. I loved putting on his favorite color.

I couldn't wait to wear the bangles on my arms.

They slipped in with ease. They were a perfect size. I purchased them without a second thought.

Sharaf came to pick us up after we were done with our shopping spree. He waited for us outside the car, leaning against the hood. He watched us cross the street from the parking lot.

We stumbled on the other side of the road with loaded bags hanging from our limbs. His sister and I talked excitedly, discussing our purchases, still on a high from our outing.

"Look at these." I laid my wrists in front of him as I showed him the blue bangles, a wide smile on my lips. "I got these specially for you."

"Hm." Sharaf spared me a glance as he put the key in the ignition.

My heart sank a little. I looked up to study his face. There were no emotions on display, but I knew him well enough to know he was deeply upset.

We were quiet the entire ride. His sister kept chatting as she failed to pick up the tension between us. We dropped her off at her in-laws soon and then started for mine.

"What's wrong?" I asked the moment we were alone again, turning my head up to look at him.

His eyes were hard. His jaw taut. Thc anger was beginning to show on his face.

He whipped his head to look at me, the expression on his face spiteful. "Take a look at what you're wearing," he said, voice sharp enough to cut steel.

I looked down. I was wearing a simple salwar kameez, loose enough to cover my curves. I had a shawl wrapped around my shoulders that covered my chest fully. I knew the scarf on my head was in place as well, a practice I had picked up right after marriage.

I met his gaze again, stumped. "What am I wearing?" I asked in return.

"Why did you decide to dress up today?" he hissed under his breath. "Why did you put on these nice clothes just to go shopping?"

I was bewildered. I couldn't understand what he was implying. "I didn't know you had an issue with the way I dressed," I told him cluelessly.

He gritted his teeth and turned to look at me, the annoyance in them as clear as the sky outside. My stomach was churning uncomfortably.

"Who was that man? Why was he staring at you?" he demanded.

I continued to stare at him helplessly. "I honestly have no idea whom you're talking about."

"Don't act like an idiot, Neela." He raised his voice, his sharp jeer slicing through my heart.

Tears were starting to well up in my eyes. "I don't know. I didn't see any man," I promised, fully starting to sob. "I was with your sister the entire time. You can ask her. I don't know why he was looking at me. I don't even know whom you were referring to."

His anger subsided as he saw my tears, my

pleading face. He was starting to cool a little. But the agitation he started in my heart was still gnawing at me.

"Fine," he said at last. "But don't dress like this again unless you're going out with me."

7. HIS

We were out at a bustling restaurant with his cousins. The place was crowded with people of all ages. As the sky kept getting darker, offices were reaching their end hours, and the pace of the restaurant kept increasing.

Sharaf had an arm loosely wrapped around my shoulder. He was relaxed, as it was the night before a long weekend. He was sneaking glances at me with those rich brown eyes between conversations, his lips curled up in a playful smile.

There was chatter going on in every direction. Sharaf was laughing and joking with his cousins. When he wanted, he could be very funny and charming. The rest of the gang was responding to him just as enthusiastically. I was still an outsider amongst his family, but his cousins were making an attempt to make me feel included. They asked me all kinds of questions. However, I kept losing my chain of thoughts as Sharaf drew small circles with subtle fingers on my arm, erupting butterflies in my stomach.

My eyes accidentally caught a gaze across the table. It was one of Sharaf's cousins. The guy was close to my husband's age and also one of his nearest friends. Our gazes clashed but only briefly. I quickly looked away, but not before he shot me a courteous smile.

"How long has it exactly been since your marriage?" he asked, leaning forward on the table, catching both mine and Sharaf's attention.

My husband looked up, confusion appearing in his eyes at the sudden question.

I expected Sharaf to respond, when he didn't, I hesitated. I wasn't used to men from outside of my family approaching me. Even when I was in university, I was known as the conservative girl so my male classmates steered clear of me. "Six months," I ended up responding, a happy smile lifting up a corner of my lip at the realization that we have made it halfway to a year.

The conversation died there. The food was served, and it was demolished in the blink of an eye. The crowd of the restaurant was starting to thin. The pace of the movement around us was starting to slow down. We, too, got up from our seats one by one, ready to go home for the night.

We bade everyone goodbye and headed for his car. I got in, and Sharaf sped down the street. My eyes were on the fleeting buildings outside the window, a lazy smile on my lips, and the colors of the city zooming past me.

A loud, angry thud startled me out of my thoughts. A soft gasp escaped my lips out of reflex, and I looked over my shoulder to meet Sharaf's eyes.

I searched for the warmth of his brown eyes, but it was nowhere to be found. The previous mellow contentment between us was now faint, my heart racing in its stead. The gaze that met me reminded me of the sky during a thunderstorm—dark and angry.

"W-what's going on?" I stuttered.

He kept his eyes on the street, refusing to look at me.

"How dare you," he seethed. "What kind of woman must you be to flirt with my own brother?"

Disbelief flashed across my face. That ugly, painful feeling started churning in my stomach again. My agitation returned. His jaw was clenched. His hands tightly clutched the steering wheel. He was fuming.

"Have you lost your mind?" I asked softly.

He slammed his hand against the steering wheel again, making me jump out of my skin this time. A slight terror peaked in my heart.

"I saw the way you were talking to him," he sneered. "The eyes you were making at him."

A heaviness pressed my heart. I could feel sobs

racking my chest. Tears were starting to pool in my eyes.

"I have never, in my entire life, looked at any other man except you without lowering my gaze," I said, voice straining.

"You were making unnecessary conversations with him," Sharaf said bitterly, his face twisting as he mentioned it. "Don't take me to be a fool."

"He asked a question," I replied between sobs. "About us. I simply responded. There was nothing else," I insisted. "You were right beside me."

He met my eyes directly, the rage in them burning my soul. His face contorted into disgust. "What kind of signals are you sending men that they feel so free to approach you?"

I was aghast. My heart was bleeding. "Wallahi, believe me," I begged. "I don't even feel comfortable conversing with men outside of my family."

We were nearing his house, but my distress was nowhere close to diminishing. His anger ensued. He kept charging me with unpleasant questions. Raising fingers at my character. It came to a point where he called me a word I could never in my worst nightmare imagine to be called, that too by my husband.

We reached home. I got out of the car, my eyes sparkling with unshed emotions. My father-in-law was in the living room watching the late-night news, and I assumed my mother-in-law was already in bed as she slept early. Though I didn't yet develop a close relationship with my in-laws and they didn't particularly show me a lot of affection, we had a cordial relationship. Usually, we'd stop for a greeting; Sharaf's father liked to ask for details of our outing, his mother would affectionately touch Sharaf's hair and ask him if he had fun. We'd linger and discuss for a little bit. However, I stepped inside the house and ran straight for our room as I was afraid I wouldn't be able to put up a front, even for the sake of social obligations. Disregarding how rude I was being, I sprinted past my father-in-law, entered the bathroom, and locked the door behind me.

"Neela." I heard Sharaf call out, his voice impatient. "Come out. Don't be a child," he said as he knocked on the door.

I let the pain in my chest flow freely again as I clutched the sink and sobbed.

He kept knocking on the door. I refused to let him in.

My parents never lost their temper with us, let alone use vulgar names. I have never seen my father raise his voice against my mother. We were treated like princesses all our lives.

His demands to open the door ceased after a while.

I let the tears stop, though my heart was still in turmoil. I splashed water to cool my aching face, then I opened the door and stepped out.

He was sitting on the bed, arms resting on his

knees, the exhaustion clear in his posture. Feeling my presence, he looked up.

Guilt was swirling in his eyes, there was pain in them as they traced over my features.

"I can't bear it when I see other men near you," he confessed, the emotion in his voice raw. "I can't stand to imagine you as anyone else's but mine."

I sat in the space beside him, the look on my face still indignant. "How could you call me that word?" I asked, the hurt clear in my voice. "Knowing completely well that I have never been with any other man but you?"

"I-I don't know what came over me." He lowered his eyes to his lap, the guilt intensifying. He reached out, touching my waist. He pulled me closer to him, meeting my eyes again. "I became so angry," he said, his voice turning hoarse. "When I even entertained the idea that you could be interested in my cousin."

"Then why did you?" I asked softly as he lowered his head to touch my forehead with his. "I have no interest in anyone else but you."

"I want you to be just mine," he breathed close to my mouth.

"I'm only yours," I promised.

And I fully tried to uphold that promise. I was only his with my heart, soul, and mind.

I remained loyal to him with my eyes, lips, and hands.

None was sufficient for him. His cousins greeted

me cordially every time they saw me, even when I avoided looking or starting conversation. Men in the streets looked in my direction even when I was with him. Vendors in stores asked for my attention every time I passed by them. I wanted to give Sharaf everything that would make him happy, but it was asking for the impossible since I had no control over how other men acted around me, and my efforts alone weren't enough for my husband.

I started becoming anxious around anyone other than him.

Still, his suspicions deepened. His tendency to control was increasing and his temper was like a ticking bomb ready to detonate any minute. I was growing miserable. Sharaf wanted me in a way I wasn't humanly capable of giving him.

seven
her

IT WAS our first wedding anniversary.

Neither Sharaf nor I were big on celebrations. He was a private person and I didn't enjoy attention, so we both decided it was better to keep it small. We planned an evening just for the two of us. We were going to eat dinner at a local restaurant and then watch a movie in our room afterward.

My mother-in-law, however, had something else in mind.

"It's your first anniversary. We want to celebrate it with you, too," she insisted.

We couldn't deny her request. She arranged a party on the roof of their house. She invited families, friends, and neighbors from both sides of the family. She carefully chose the menu and then single-handedly spent three days cooking every item. What started as a small intimate affair between husband

and wife became an atrocious matter, including all members of the community.

I could tell Sharaf was unhappy. I was uncomfortable with the whole matter as well. Despite that, we accepted my mother-in-law's efforts graciously to avoid hurting her feelings.

I wanted to look nice for my husband, regardless of the unfavorable situation. I wore a blue sharee, his color of choice. I applied basic makeup and took out the blue bangles I got at the mall all those months ago. As I was getting ready, I heard his footsteps approaching.

I briskly stopped what I was doing and met his eyes. He merely greeted me with a kiss on the forehead, then he headed to the bathroom. I resumed the task at hand and continued to slide in the bangles on my wrists when I heard his phone buzz on my dresser.

I looked down, purely out of instinct. That's when I saw her name flashing on the screen.

eight
anger

I WAS STARING at her name, my heart painfully racing against my chest.

Why was a woman, whom I didn't know, texting my husband?

I tried to calm myself down. I told myself I was overreacting over a simple text. But my husband always boasted with confidence that he barely socialized with women outside of the family and told me I should do the same if I wanted to remain a loyal wife. I couldn't fathom it. I failed to reason with myself. My heart started palpitating.

He reentered the room, jerking me out of my thoughts. I glanced at him through the mirror. The distress in my eyes was completely lost on him. Sharaf simply reached over my shoulder to get to the dresser and picked up his phone.

We were soon called upstairs. The guests arrived.

The evening passed by in a blur. The greetings, the congratulations, and even the subtle touches of my husband went over my head. My mind refused to let me forget the name, painfully dangling it in front of me every time I looked at Sharaf.

We were celebrating our marriage, and my heart was dying.

All I kept thinking about was the woman texting my husband.

I couldn't even bear to start entertaining the reasons behind it.

It wasn't until deep into the night, when we were alone and in our room, that I confronted him.

"Who's she?"

My voice was calm and steady, yet the question threw him off the loop. He looked up from his phone, his face aghast.

"What?" he asked.

"I saw her text on your phone."

I watched as numerous emotions flickered on his face. He was shocked at first, which turned to guilt and then distress. I had never seen Sharaf this overwhelmed. He finally landed on nonchalance.

"She's a colleague," he replied coolly.

He didn't deny knowing her. The last bit of hope I was holding onto seemed to slip through my fingers. I felt my world topple.

"Why is she texting you?" My eyes searched his face, my heart breaking anew.

"She's a colleague, Neela," he replied tiredly. "She had a work-related question."

I couldn't believe him. My face was full of incredulity as I stared at him. "It doesn't matter," I cried, my voice straining. "Why are you talking to a woman?"

His face twisted into rage real quick. "Is that doubt I hear in your voice?" he seethed. "Are you questioning my character?"

I was trembling, the pain in my heart overtaking me. I barely felt in control of the reins of my own emotions. "I don't know," I replied with a strained voice.

"Here," he spat, throwing his phone into my lap. "See for yourself if that satisfies you."

I picked up the phone, knowing full well that it was only provoking him further. Sharaf looked at me with shock again—he didn't think I'd actually touch his phone. But I didn't care. The only thing that mattered was to learn whether my husband was involved with another woman.

I scrolled through his phone. Checked the messages. I found the particular text. Sharaf was telling the truth, but he wasn't.

It was posted in a group chat. There were plenty of people there that I didn't know—his colleagues—the part of his life I wasn't even allowed to ask about. There were women and men alike. I started skimming the messages. They were all talking to each other casually, joking, sometimes even addressing one another individually—that included my husband, too. The conversations were completely platonic.

It was nothing, but it was everything.

"S-some of these messages are months old," I fumbled with my words.

"They're as old as I have worked for that company," was his curt reply.

I looked up, eyes full of tears. I felt like I was seeing my husband for the first time. He's the man who laughed and joked with his female colleagues about things I wasn't even aware of.

I searched his face. He was holding onto that stubborn anger. The part of me that doubted his character had been put to sleep, but a new beast was waking in my heart, and it was just as unpleasant.

"I'm not allowed to breathe around my male cousins, and you have inside jokes with your female colleagues?"

His gaze did not waver for a second, but his Adam's apple bobbed up and down subtly. That was the only indication that he was uncomfortable.

"It's not the same," he replied briskly.

"It is exactly the same thing." I was crying, unable to hold back the flood of emotions.

"Are you trying to find an excuse to talk to other men?" he spewed through gritted teeth, roughly grabbing my hand that was clutching his phone. "Is that what it is?"

That wrath in his eyes flickered fear in my heart like it always did.

"N-no," I stuttered again.

He brought his face closer to mine, his warm breath coating my face, "then why are we talking about this?"

I pulled hard to free my arm from his grasp. I leaned back to get a direct view of his eyes again. "We're talking about it because you called me a prostitute for answering a simple question asked by your cousin, you did not talk to me for two days for laughing at a joke made by your friend, and you have banned me from even standing in front of our window in case one of our neighbors see me," I spewed back.

Sharaf blinked at me, astounded to see me standing my ground for the first time. Part of me was surprised as well, but what I knew I felt wholeheartedly was outrage.

"I'm not okay with this. I won't allow it," I said vehemently.

He didn't know how to act. He had never seen me angry.

"Fine," he finally hissed under his breath.

He reached out for his phone still in my clutches. Sharaf pressed a few buttons and carelessly placed the phone aside. "I deleted the chat. It's done," he informed curtly. "And I'll maintain a distance from my colleagues if that's what you want."

nine
lies

WE FINALLY WENT on the honeymoon we never got.

When we got married, we did not have the financial capacity to splurge on a trip like this. But after Sharaf had been in the workforce for over a year, and making an effort to save up, we were finally able to afford it.

We spent weeks choosing the place, deciding our itinerary, and booking the hotels. Of course, all the details were handled by him. When all was confirmed and the time came, we packed our bags and flew to the Maldives.

I was beyond excited. I had never stepped a foot outside of my own city. I stared with awe as my eyes caught large crowds of people consisting of numerous cultures and races.

Our hotel was more luxurious than anything I had

ever experienced in my life. I squealed with delight as soon as I stepped into our room. I sprinted through the open doors of the balcony facing the majestic ocean.

"Look at the view!" I gushed, my eyes darting between the blue sea below and the open sky above, and not being able to decide which I wanted to look at more.

Sharaf chuckled from behind. I heard him take steps towards me. Soon, he wrapped his arms around my waist and pulled me closer to his body, his fingers lacing over my stomach.

"How can I look at anything else when you're in front of me?"

His voice was a whisper, and it tickled my ears. I let out a chuckle at his words. I knew, even without looking, that there was a playful look in his brown eyes. Warmth spread in my chest and butterflies erupted in my stomach at the contentment of the situation. With the blue water as witness, I could have lived in that moment forever.

I woke up to the soothing lullaby of the sea.

The first thing I noticed was that it was still dark. My eyes drifted to Sharaf to find him peacefully sleeping besides me. I gently rolled to my side and got to my feet quietly. I wrapped a loose blanket around my shoulders, and my eyes locked on the view outside. I walked towards the balcony and leaned against the door frame, marveling at its beauty.

It was still too early for anyone to be up. I watched the waves lap restlessly over the soft, grainy shore. I felt the fresh breeze dance around, slightly salty from the sea. I stared and wondered what it would be like to be as restless as the sea or as free as the breeze. I felt the sudden desire to let go of the bindings holding me and run with the waves carried by the free wind.

I heard Sharaf stir in his sleep. I let out a heavy breath and twirled on my bare feet, my eyes lingering on the view for a few more seconds. I looked at my sleeping husband. I was about to return to bed when I heard his phone buzz. I withdrew my arm and sauntered toward our bedside table, where his phone was, with a frown. It was an inappropriate time for anyone to be calling or messaging him, even if they lived in the time zone of our hometown.

I picked it up and stared at the texts, speechless.

Bits and pieces of conversations started circulating in my head: all those nights he had to work late, the flimsy excuses to skip dinner at home, the 'business' trip he recalled only at the last minute. My heart unpleasantly trembled, my fingers shaking.

The brightening phone screen chilled the blood in my veins.

ten
loop

SHARAF WAS WOKEN from his slumber with the adhan for fajr prayer ringing from his phone and echoing across the room. He fluttered his eyes open and rested his upper body on his elbows. His gaze landed on me as I sat with his phone cradled in my hands, my agitated heart unharmoniously racing against the soothing call for prayer.

Whether it was the dead look in my eyes or the tautness of my jaw, Sharaf knew I had seen what he had not intended for my gaze.

The group chat he left and deleted—solemnly swearing off—was still buzzing, alive, and completely accessible through his phone. The months of texts consisted of details of hangouts, lunch outings, and impromptu dinners. Worst of all, there were hundreds of photos from a trip outside of the city—

Sharaf laughing with his buddies in all of them—none of which I had any idea about.

"Neela," he started.

"Don't," I warned, my voice already starting to tremble.

"What are you wearing?" he hissed.

I turned to look at him, my eyes desperate. "How could you lie to me like this? How could you break your promise to me?" I cried.

"What the hell are you wearing?" he snarled, roughly pulling himself into a sitting position with the help of his arms.

"Nothing!" I shouted, losing the last bit of my patience and glowering at him with all my being. "I'm wearing absolutely nothing except the blanket we slept with last night."

His eyes turned hard. He clenched his teeth so hard there was a tic on his jaw.

"Go put on decent attire first if you want me to take you seriously," he snorted, beckoning with his hand towards the bathroom.

"You will tell me, right now, what these photos and messages mean," I spat out each word.

He stared at me, eyes as angry as the sky during a thunderstorm. I stared back this time, mine as restless as the sea. He was slightly jarred by the way my unwavering gaze met his. I wasn't looking away; his temper tantrums weren't buckling my will. I demanded answers—and I wasn't letting him escape my questions this time.

Sharaf let out a sigh, his rage diffusing. He wiped his face of any emotions. "They mean what you think they mean," he said vaguely, nonchalance rolling off of him.

"You lied to me for months," I stated, my voice deflating, tears rolling from my eyes. "You told me you were working. I stayed up for you night after night as our dinner turned cold when the truth is you have just been sneaking out to hang out with your friends—most of them female."

"What do you expect me to do, huh?" he barked. "This is how it works when you go out to work. You have to socialize with your teammates, even if they're female. Do you want me to sit at home and become a hermit?"

"If they're just colleagues, why did you lie to me about it?" I asked, sobbing.

"Because you become an irrational person when you hear about my life outside of the house," he responded. "I have tried including you in my friends' circle or telling you about my colleagues, but you simply don't get it. You even cried like a child the last time you found my texts with them. Sometimes I feel like I can't even breathe around you freely."

I stared at him, dumbfounded, wondering if he were truly as blind and dense as the words spitting out of his mouth.

"I cried like a child because this is exactly how you would have acted if it were me, instead of you, making male friends and going on trips with them," I said, voice turning sharp enough to cut steel. "God, you would have handled it much worse."

His expression changed in a split second. From cold and stoic, he became enraged and burning. "How dare you?" he hissed, reaching out to snatch the phone from my hands. "How dare you even think of such a thing?" He threw his phone to the other side of the room.

The phone hit the floor on the other side of the room. I jerked in my seat at the splitting crack.

"You want to be with other men. That's what it is, isn't it?"

I grabbed my hair out of pure exasperation. The frustration I felt in my chest was stronger than anything I had ever felt in my life. We kept having the same conversation over and over again, hurling words at each other in a loop that the other couldn't hear.

I looked up, eyes defeated, shoulders slumped. "That's not what this is about," I said, voice strained. "I have no desire to be with anyone else but you. Yet, no matter how many times I have proven this, you act like an insane person, blaming me every time a man comes near me. But you freely mix with your female colleagues, even though it's not something I'm comfortable with. How do you expect me to be okay with this?"

He let out a sigh, displeasure simmering behind his eyes. Sharaf descended from the bed and started putting on his clothes, his movements quick and hasty.

"I can't deal with you right now," he muttered under his breath. Then, carelessly picking up his phone, he headed towards the door.

My eyes bore on his back, wondering if he truly were the man I fell in love with on the moonlit night on my rooftop.

eleven
tears

WE RETURNED HOME a couple of days later.

Sharaf was gone for hours after our fight in the Maldives. I was terrified, not only because of the fragile state of our marriage but also because I disliked being completely by myself, even back home, let alone in a foreign country.

It was late at night when Sharaf returned to our room, and he completely shut away from me. He barely made eye contact and didn't even bother to tell me where he was. I was too upset to pry an answer from him. His cold indifference slowly turned to anger. As we were stepping out of the plane, he was furious with me for ruining our honeymoon. He placed the entire blame for the fight on my shoulders, chiding me for overreacting to the simplest things.

I didn't console, reason, or argue back. I stayed quiet the entire time, my mind the exact opposite.

My heart was caught in a battle I wasn't sure it would survive.

Upon returning, I curtly requested him to take me to my parents' house. He didn't object. In fact, he seemed relieved at the idea of the space my departure would provide him.

He drove me to my house the next morning, his fancy car standing out in the dingy street where I grew up, and he sped away with it as soon as I stepped down without even saying goodbye.

I hadn't spent a single night at my own home, or away from Sharaf for that matter, since we got married—with the exception of the two nights he had spent with his friends on that trip.

My heart was in turmoil. Despite our fight, I missed my husband. I missed his kisses and his fingers running through my hair in the middle of the night. But I knew we needed the space. I reminded myself of the anger and the frustration I felt for all those months, and I held onto them.

My one-night stay at my parents extended to a few more. I told my mother Sharaf had an important deadline to meet so he requested me to stay with my family for a few days as he needed the space to work. It wasn't exactly a lie since I knew my husband wanted time away from me, but it was a flimsy excuse. However, since I said I was away from home upon his request, my parents didn't protest.

I was lying on my bed one of those evenings. I

was back in the room I shared with my sister growing up. All these years, this is the room that felt like home to me. The place I craved to return to no matter where I was. But that was no longer the case; I wasn't sure *if* I had a home anymore. I was feeling blue. I kept thinking of those brown eyes. I saw Billu saunter into the room, his tail high and his rear moving in a posh rhythm.

"C'mon, Billu," I called out to him softly. "Come sleep with me."

The cat jumped on the bed in one fluid movement. He curled himself into a ball near my pillow and snuggled close, giving me a face full of his tail.

A small smile made its way to my lips. My sister and I always used to complain about the nawab cat's tendency to shove its butt into our faces every time we asked it to snuggle with us, even though we told him repeatedly not to.

But I didn't even mind it this time. I fondly dug my fingers into his soft fur and shifted his position so my face would meet a more appropriate body part. My heart recalled just how much I loved and missed this snooty cat.

I snuggled him closer to my chest, burying my face over his head. "Sleep with me tonight, Billu," I murmured against his fur. "I don't have to hide my tears from you."

twelve
realization

AS THE DAYS ESCALATED, my stay at home was starting to raise suspicions.

Relatives were asking questions when they visited our house. My mother was beginning to look distraught as she informed them of the length of my stay.

It wasn't appropriate for a girl to spend so much time away from her husband's house without a justified cause.

My sister whispered to me one night, "Are you guys okay?"

I had no answer to that.

The next day, my mother asked me with concern, "When are you returning to your home, Neela?"

Her question was met with silence as well.

One rainy evening, my mother requested that I

drop my sister off at her college. She insisted it was because she didn't want my younger sister to travel alone, even though she perfectly used to traveling by public transport by herself. My mom's feeble excuse was enough for me to understand that she was sending me out of the house because she didn't want to face the incoming guest's unpleasant queries.

I went to get dressed anyway. I was still living off the suitcase I had brought with me, and it was becoming painfully obvious that I was a guest overstaying her welcome. I had been repeating the same clothes over and over as I had not planned to stay as long as I was.

I examined the contents of my suitcase. The only color smiling back at me was blue. It wrenched my heart with pain, reminding me of those brown eyes I couldn't bear to think about these days. I tried to look for a different color and, with a startling realization, discovered that I had none. I began to wonder when and how I had only started to wear blue.

The answer came to me simply: since I married Sharaf and because it was his favorite color. I was taken back to the first day I had met him at the fair. He had brought me the blue scarf without asking if I had any preferences, marking me as his from the first sight.

I tried to recall if he had once asked me what my favorite color was. For a moment, I wondered if I even had one or if I had lost so much of myself to him that I no longer did.

My weeks of stay turned into months. Sharaf did not call me once to ask me to return. And I was starting to wonder if I wanted to at all.

thirteen
reassessment

MY MOTHER'S distress was reaching a peak when Sharaf showed up at our house.

I found him sitting in my parents' minimally decorated living space, looking completely out of place. Sharaf's expression was unreadable. His shirt was too formal, his hair too fancy, his watch very expensive.

My heart wrenched with pain as my eyes met his. I drank in his features—his eyes, nose, hair. My first instinct was to sprint into his arms, embrace him tightly, and never let go. But I reeled in my desire.

I took a seat beside him, his eyes following my every movement with a frown between his brows. My father was at work, and my mother was in the next room, brimming with excitement as she believed my husband was here to take me back to my in-laws. My sister and Billu were locked up with her as well to allow Sharaf and I to have our discussion without interruptions.

"Why haven't you come home yet, Neela?" he hissed. "People are starting to ask questions."

I looked at him. He was annoyed. He was pissed. I was starting to recall my frustration.

"Do *you* want me to?" I whispered, my eyes searching his.

"What kind of question is this?" he spat. "It has been weeks. You didn't even bother to call me once."

"You didn't answer my question."

My voice was calm and steady. His eyes were the exact opposite.

He let out a sigh of annoyance. "You're my wife," he snapped. "You're supposed to be by my side. What kind of woman spends so much time away from her husband?"

Storm and dark—that's all I saw in his eyes. None of the warmth of the rich brown that had won my heart. That I fell in love with.

"What were you thinking, Neela?" he scoffed.

I tried to think of a time when my husband didn't constantly point fingers at my character and failed. I thought of how relieved I felt for the past few months because I didn't have to live with the mental pressure he put on me when other men looked at me. I recalled my wardrobe and the blue clothes. What he wanted and liked, and what others thought about him—that's all that mattered to him. Even now, he was more worried about his reputation than the condition of our relationship. Did he even care about me? Us?

The answer that popped into my head broke my heart. I let out a labored sigh.

"I—I can't do this anymore," I told him.

fourteen
restlessness

HE STARED at me with utter confusion.

"You what?" he spat.

My heart raced in a way I couldn't explain, my soul fighting to crawl out of the prison it was bound in.

"I can't do this anymore," I repeated. Clear and loud. "This is too difficult."

He let out a scoff. "What do you mean by that?"

My eyes searched his, desperately trying to find even a semblance of kindness in them. But my husband held none for me.

"I—I don't know," I replied, drifting my eyes away from him. The disappointment in his gaze was already buckling my will. "All I know is that I don't want to go back with you," I managed to mutter.

"You really love to drag things out, don't you?" he

snorted. “We had one pesky fight, and now you don’t want to return home.”

“It’s not about that one fight,” I cried, my patience starting to wear thin. “It’s everything,” I told him. “Including your stubborn refusal to acknowledge our problems.”

“I don’t have time for this,” he muttered, pinching the bridge of his nose in exasperation. “Just pack your bags and come with me,” he said, turning to me again.

I stared at him, resentment beginning to bloom in my heart. It cemented into a determination I didn’t know I was capable of.

“I’m not going anywhere,” I said, my tone resilient. “I meant what I said. I have no intention of returning anytime soon. I can’t deal with you anymore.”

He studied me for a while, clear denial in his eyes.

“We’ll see about that,” he said as he got to his feet to step towards the door.

The next few days carried the weight of a few years.

Sharaf’s parents called mine, informing them of my refusal to return to my in-laws.

My mother started wailing.

“What do you mean to achieve by this, Neela?”

she shouted at me. "What kind of a woman refuses to return to her husband's home?"

I couldn't come up with an appropriate response to the question. All I could think about was how the idea of living with him again was starting to suffocate me.

Sharaf's parents arrived at my house. The elders were called for a meeting to hear the reasoning behind my stance. The couple of times my in-laws have visited my parents they always seemed uncomfortable and spent as little time with them as possible. Though they shared a cordial relationship with my family, they belonged to a different class of society so there was very little that was common between the two sets of parents. However, that evening my in-laws spent hours in my house – discussing

The idea of baring my heart to the entire family, the intimate contents of my marriage, was the worst thing I could think of. I started dreading ever opening my mouth.

Nervousness and anxiety demolished my gut as I sat to tell my story. In the room, apart from Sharaf and me, were the two pairs of parents. My mother was so nervous she could barely sit. My father, on the other hand, sat as silent as a mountain—an indication that he was deeply upset. Both of Sharaf's parents looked anxious.

The words were hard to form at first, and the emotions were hard to keep in check. The thought of speaking about the contents of my marital life in front of the elders felt like a violation of my privacy. But once I got into the flow, I couldn't stop. The months of pain and endurance, everything I had bottled up in my heart, was relieving to let go of, even liberating.

I told them everything—his disregard of my feelings, his possessiveness, his constant lies and deceit.

The parents were staring at me with furrowed eyebrows by the end of it.

"Dear," his mother sighed. "I get it. it seems to you now that this marriage is impossible," she said. "But take it from someone who has been married for over thirty years: these are all minor issues that can be solved just by talking to your spouse."

"I can't," I said, my voice thick with emotion, exasperated beyond belief. "I have tried to talk to him repeatedly. It's—" I swallowed. "It's like we don't even speak the same language."

She pursed her lips. "Then you have to try harder, sweetie. Do you think I have sustained my marriage without overcoming such difficulties?"

"Neela," his father started. "These things happen, sweetheart. Such situations must be dealt with patience. You can't make hasty decisions based on fights or fleeting emotions."

I blinked at them, my eyes darting from one clueless face to another.

I wanted to tell them that my actions weren't

based on one incident. My broken heart wasn't the result of whimsical emotions. Months of pain, anguish, and denial of peace had led me to this. His tendency to belittle me and doubt my character constantly had turned me bitter.

The elders sent me to my room with my father's deeply disapproving eyes boring into my back. My mother followed me out.

"You're upset with your husband because of female colleagues?" she asked in a harsh whisper. "These things are normal for today's men, Neela! You can't expect your husband to not talk to any other woman."

I kept quiet, knowing any kind of explanation would only lead to a worse argument.

My mother hurried back to join the other parents. I sat on my bed, and began to reassess everything I said and felt

fifteen
hope

MY DAYS WENT by in confusion, distress, and turmoil. The news of my overstay at my parents' house spread in the community. Our friends and family started speculating about the state of my marriage.

My parents were in a frenzy. People took the liberty to throw unpleasant questions at me. I was eyed with distrust at every event.

My entire family was getting ready to go to a wedding one evening. I watched as my sister excitedly spent time choosing her attire, put on a beautiful dress, and adorned her wrists with bangles.

Our family had been shut and traumatized for days, so this was needed. A break. A chance to provide everyone an opportunity to distract themselves.

My mother entered the room, and the familiar

look of resentment descended on her face. "Make sure to lock the house after we leave," she said curtly.

I meekly nodded, averting my eyes elsewhere as I couldn't bear to see the disappointment in her gaze. I peeked at my sister again, longing rising to my chest for things I wasn't allowed to desire anymore. I wondered if I'd ever get the opportunity to attend a wedding again.

It was decided I wouldn't accompany my family as nobody wanted my mess around when they were celebrating their happiness; nobody wanted the girl whose relationship was falling apart to pass on her bad fortune to the newly married couple. Separation of marriage was too big of a taboo. I was deemed inauspicious.

My family left for the wedding, and I locked myself in, alone for the first time in a while. I used to hate being by myself, but this time, it felt like I was given a chance to breathe.

I spent the evening with Billu. The cat took turns to play with his soft toys and cuddle with me. It was around Isha prayer that I felt the need to go out and get some fresh air.

I contemplated it. Going out of the house provided the chance to walk into someone unkind. My parents would be angry if they knew I had gone out alone. But I couldn't resist the desire to breathe in freely. I put out enough food for Billu's dinner, the cat could be by himself for a few hours when he had his basic needs taken care of, clothed myself in a scarf and abaya and left my house.

The evening was chilly, promising of rain. The damp air was liberating—a stark contrast to the stuffy room I was in. This was the first time since my marriage that I had gone out by myself. I watched the people on the streets as I walked by, moving about in their usual lives. I stared with longing as I saw them laugh at the most mundane things, wondering what I wouldn't give to be this carefree again.

I strolled close to the sidewalk. Amidst the busy street, something caught my eye. I saw our local mosque, upright and pristine white, standing out in the polluted environment. Something stirred in my chest at the sight, reigniting a dormant hope within me.

I took hesitant steps towards the mosque, entering it after however many years I didn't even know. The women's section was relatively empty like it always was. Only a few women were sparsely seated here and there. The congregational prayer had just ended, so the ladies who were there were either uttering supplications or working in the mosque.

I timidly sat in one corner, feeling out of place, my heart heavy. I raised my hands in prayer, and the unbearable anguish of my heart started pouring through my eyes. Before I knew it, I was sobbing. I was crying like I never had before. I felt like my chest was going to tear and wrench itself out of my body.

I lost track of how long I sat there crying. All I knew was that I was hurting, and I wanted this chaos to end. I wanted to pray for something, but I couldn't form words, so I just sat there and cried.

A hand touched my shoulder, breaking me out of my trance and rooting me back to the earth. I looked up, eyes still full of torment, and found an older woman staring back at me.

She was clearly from a wealthier family, that is the first thing I noticed. Her abaya, scarf, and purse did not look like they belonged to this part of the town. She was older, her eyes wise, and face full of kindness I hadn't experienced in a while.

"What's wrong, daughter?" she asked, "I've been watching you for a while."

I turned away from her gaze, taking the time to wipe my tears and clean my face.

My first instinct was to say, "Nothing," but the heaviness in my heart prevented me from lying. It wasn't nothing, and the aching in my chest was too heavy to be denied. "I'm going through something," I told her.

"What is it?" she pressed.

"I don't think my marriage is going to work out," I confessed aloud for the first time, my voice tired and dull.

The moment the words left my lips, the moment I realized what I had done, I turned to look at the woman again. Without even giving her a chance to react, my face turned to resentment. I felt an irrational anger towards her.

"I'll take my leave," I told her, my tone clipped. "It's getting late."

I was about to get up when she held my hand. "Wait, wait," she said, taken aback by my sudden harsh reaction. "Just give me a moment to tell you what I have to say."

My eyes hardened. "No, thank you," I said bitterly. "I've heard enough from people."

I got to my feet and was about to turn. "Daughter, wait," she pleaded. "I was once a divorced woman as well."

sixteen
deliberation

I SAT TALKING to the woman for a long time.

The mosque got emptier, the night deeper—but the contents of our hearts were never-ending.

"I was young when I met him," she started. "Still a teen. We were introduced through our families and married off soon after. I learned quickly enough that he was emotionally unstable," she paused. "I don't remember when the beatings started, but I remember it was unbearable. I begged my family to let me come back home, but they kept refusing. Women in my family did not get divorced," she let out a heavy sigh. "After a near-death experience and a bruise I'm still wearing, I decided I had enough and left him for good."

"How did you go through with the divorce?" I asked, eyes searching for answers. "How did you survive?"

"It wasn't easy," she replied, eyes recalling days she would rather keep buried. "It's still the hardest thing I have ever done. Understand that those times were different, people cared more about a family's honor than a person's well-being. I could have never survived it if a kinder man hadn't taken my responsibility." A small smile appeared on her lips. "He was a neighbor. He was always nice to me. He married me soon after, and we have been together ever since."

"My husband never hurt me physically, but around him, I find it even difficult to breathe."

"Tell me more about him, your relationship," she said.

"I barely knew him before we got married. The marriage took place in a rush because my parents were afraid my brief association with him would hurt my reputation." I let out a sigh. "For a while, I thought I could love him, start a family with him." At the mention of that, a deep desire burned in my chest. Having my own family and children was something I desperately wanted. "But I'm starting to think maybe he wasn't ready to get married at all."

"Daughter, do you think staying in the marriage is the best option for both of you?"

I dropped my gaze on my interlaced fingers. "I—I don't know."

"Then that's what you need to figure out. A relationship cannot continue in this manner. You need to find a way to communicate your feelings, be heard, and come to a decision."

I looked up, my desperate eyes searching for an answer. "How?"

"Hm," she let out a thoughtful sigh. "I know this man. He is an imam of a mosque. He is wise and compassionate and has worked as an arbitrator for many couples I know. I think he could help you out as well."

With a goodbye and the man's phone number, I left for my home again.

seventeen
decision

MY PARENTS WERE OVERCOME with renewed enthusiasm when I informed them that I wanted to seek out an arbitrator to sort out the issues in my marriage. My father wasted no time to set an appointment with the man. My mother started meeting my eyes and speaking to me once more.

My parents, along with Sharaf and his, showed up at the address to meet the arbitrator. After asr prayer, we were led to a small office behind the prayer area. He was an average looking middle-aged man, eyes shining with wisdom.

He introduced himself as the imam of the mosque, and he spoke highly of the woman who referred us to him. While he spewed the introductions, my eyes drifted towards my husband. Sharaf had his gaze trained ahead, his face stoic, yet the subtle frown between his brows was not lost on me. I knew he was secretly furious.

Then, the man turned his focus on us. He asked Sharaf and me to share our issues. A deep silence followed as I expected my husband to take the lead, but when he stubbornly refused to speak, I started talking with a meek voice, my hope already deflated.

I told him everything I had already shared with our parents. Sharaf maintained his silence the entire time.

After I was done, the man shifted his gaze towards my husband. "Son, do you want to add anything?"

"No."

The imam furrowed his eyebrows. "In that case, I have to take your wife's word for it."

The arbitrator started by emphasizing the importance of respect in marriage. He said a woman must respect her husband, but a man needs to be kind and respectful to her too. He told Sharaf that, like it is a woman's duty to obey her husband, a man's duty is to be compassionate with his wife. Blaming her for the actions of other men, especially when she attempts to maintain hijab, was not right.

He then said it is a husband's duty to uphold his wife's trust and a wife's duty to trust her husband; and this included that men and women were equally expected to be loyal to their spouses.

The discussion carried on for a while. I was asked

for more details. Our parents were requested to chip in as well. The imam briefly elaborated on the difference between being protective and controlling.

After the meeting was over, the arbitrator told us that Sharaf and I needed to sit and have a serious discussion between us. We had to figure out exactly what is it that we wanted from each other and write it down before the next meeting. His eyes drifted toward Sharaf whenever he emphasized communication.

We left his office. As we headed towards our respective cars, our parents in the lead, I looked at my husband again. I could feel the disapproval and anger radiating off of him. My heart sank further into my stomach.

"Sharaf..."

The words died on my lips. I didn't know what to say. Helplessness was shining in my eyes.

He looked at me for the first time since the meeting. I expected to be met with either thunder and storm or impenetrable walls, like I did every time I tried to make him understand my feelings, but what I saw in his brown eyes was disappointment.

"You involved a third party in our marriage, Neela? Really?"

"I was out of options," I tried to reason. "We tried solving it ourselves, but that didn't work."

"Do you think the way to solve issues in a marriage is to speak ill about your spouse in front of a stranger?" he scolded. "Is this how you think relationships work?"

I stared at him, my bleeding heart and restless, mind numbed with emotions.

"You left me with no other choice."

The hardness in his eyes melted. I saw anguish replace it.

"I don't know how to communicate with you anymore. Has it once occurred to you that this relationship is as difficult for me as it is for you?"

"This is why we need help, Sharaf," I said, my voice close to pleading. "He can help us see each other's view."

"I can't speak about our problems in front of an outsider." He ran a hand through his hair, letting out a sigh. Then, he looked at me accusingly. "I thought you knew how important privacy is to me."

I was left with a feeling of deep shame after the conversation.

But I didn't give up. The marriage counseling sowed a renewed hope for our relationship in my heart so I tried to convince Sharaf to continue sessions with the arbitrator. I wanted to believe we could work out our issues and have a marriage without the possessiveness, constant accusations, and secrets.

Sharaf refused to attend the sessions.

I was starting to get tired. I called him one night. I wondered if he could hear the pain in my voice.

"I beg you, Sharaf," I told him. "I just want to see some effort from your end. That's all."

"It is impossible to keep you happy," he hissed.

"Don't," I pleaded. "Don't do this. Don't treat me this way. If we continue down this path, then I'm afraid the damage to this relationship will be irrevocable. We're doomed to end in a div-divorce." It almost caused me physical pain to utter the last word.

There was stunned silence on his end. The silence was too quiet, too calm. Then, the storm caused havoc. "You have some nerve," he spat out. "I never took you to be the kind of woman who would utter such a word, but I was clearly mistaken. Your parents were the ones desperate to get me to marry you in the first place. They knew I didn't want to tie the knot anytime soon. Your mother literally begged mine. Your father pleaded. Yet, I married you," he said like he was doing me some kind of favor. "I accepted you. I loved you. *You* failed to keep me happy and keep up with my lifestyle. On what basis do you ask me for divorce?" he challenged.

I didn't respond for a while. I couldn't form the words to. Tears were rolling down my face quietly. The heartbreak my husband's words caused that day was unlike anything I had ever experienced. Every single word acted as a bullet to shatter the illusion that my he valued me or respected my family.

I simply hung up the phone.

I made no effort to contact him or arrange any meeting since then; my self-respect didn't allow me. A tiny, idiotic part of me still hoped that perhaps he would finally realize and make an effort to mend things. But that part died eventually as well.

It was late when I called him one more time.

"Hello?" he said.

I could hear the sleepiness in his voice. I hoped he wouldn't be able to detect the restlessness in mine.

"I want a divorce," I told him.

eighteen
suffocation

WHAT UNFOLDED NEXT WAS the stuff of my nightmare.

My father had gone silent. My mother's cries could be heard from the neighbor's house. Our families were devastated. Our parents tried to convince me to change my mind. Sometimes with love and affection, other times with harsh words.

"Have you lost your mind, girl?" my mother demanded.

"Do you understand the consequence of what you asked, Neela?" my mother-in-law tried to reason.

I wanted to tell them that I did, I wanted to shout from the top of my lungs to show them the depth of my frustration. I wish I could explain the level of pain I endured that had led me to this decision—yet even the thought of it still broke my heart.

One morning, Sharaf came to see me.

He was sitting in my room this time. My mother ushered me after him and would have locked us together in there if she had her way.

He looked different. He wasn't angry. The storm was gone. But the darkness still lingered. He looked at me, anguish and disbelief coating his face.

"Are you actually going through with this, Neela?" he asked, voice hoarse.

My heart started racing at his sight, but not in the pleasant way it used to.

I swallowed, scrambling to find my resolution.

"Yes," I replied.

"I don't understand. How could you do this?" he asked, tone accusing. "How could you even think of such a thing?"

That resentment was peeking into my chest again, anger simmered beneath my skin.

"How could you call me a prostitute or lie to me about your colleagues?" I retorted coolly.

He winced at my words. Surprise flickered in his eyes when he saw I wasn't crying or pleading. I simply sat adamantly. Next, he did something I never saw him doing. Sharaf started crying. He dropped his head over his cupped hands as his body trembled, tears leaking from his eyes.

I stared at him dumbfounded.

"I'm trying, Neela. For once, I wish you would see that."

I reached out unsurely and ran my fingers through

his soft hair, comforting him despite the distraught of my own heart.

He let his hands drop and wrapped his arms around me, pulling me closer as he burrowed his head in my chest, shaking as he cried.

"Why are you giving up on us like this?"

"I just can't do it anymore," I said, my voice straining with, my fingers still weaving between his locks of hair. I could feel the warmth of his skin. His touch used to feel loving, exciting, and as familiar as my own, but now it only reminded me of painful memories.

"They mean nothing to me," he said between sobs. "My colleagues — those people mean nothing to me."

A few weeks ago, this was all I wanted—for Sharaf to make an effort, for his heart to soften towards me. I thought it was still what I wanted, but I couldn't let go of the resentment. I held him, soothed him. I wondered if my soul had died.

"It's too late. Too much has happened between us. Too much bitterness has built up."

He looked up, lost, his eyes swollen and face red. He raised his hands to my face, gently grabbing my cheeks.

"It doesn't have to be this way." He stared into my eyes. "I'll do anything. You wanted a family, right?" he asked. "I'm ready." There was a crazed desperation in his gaze. "We can start trying for a baby as soon as you want."

A rancid taste filled my mouth at the mention of a child. The fact that Sharaf would torment me with something I wanted so desperately was a painful slap to my face. I never imagined my husband could stoop this low. I began to wonder if he had been this purposely obtuse and so disrespectful of my feelings from the beginning. If so, how did I endure it for so long? How did I not see it?

"This isn't fair," I said, removing his hands from me.

"But this is what you wanted, right?"

I shook my head. "No, not anymore."

"Then what is it that you want, my love?" he asked with despair.

"I told you already. I want a divorce."

The words shattered him; I could tell by the way he was looking at me. There was a fresh batch of tears in his eyes.

"But I love you."

I got out of his hold and got to my feet, away from him. I let my eyes wander over his features one last time.

Lost, desperate, fragmented.

Without another word, I quickly spun on my heels and sauntered towards the door, not daring to look over my shoulder even once.

My mother came to see me immediately after.

"He wants you back. He wants to make it work!" she shouted. "Why are you being this way?"

"I can't do it, Maa," I said, defeated and weary. "The idea of going back to his life—enduring his over-possessiveness, his lies, his constant disrespect—makes me feel suffocated."

She stared at me with absolute resentment. "Where did I go wrong in raising you?" she spat.

I closed my eyes momentarily. "I don't know," I sighed. "All I know is that marriage is losing its appeal to me. He dictated how I ate, slept, and breathed—then found a way to belittle *me* when called out for his unpleasant tendencies. I can't take it anymore."

The slap rang in my ears before it registered in my brain. My face was turned to the side, my cheek stinging from the contact. I straightened to face my mother again, stunned. She was staring back at me, eyes full of loathing. I couldn't believe it. The woman who never used harsh words with me before all of a sudden slapped me.

"You have brought nothing but shame on this family."

I snapped.

"I have brought shame on you?" I cried. "You married me off to a family you barely knew just to have people stop talking about me. You blindly gave me away to a man who wasn't ready for it. You continue to force me to live with him, knowing he mistreats me. Fine, you want to send me back? Do it," I challenged, tears welling up in my eyes as I made wild hand gestures. "But when I die of suffocation, and I will, then you can decide which is worse to deal with—a dead daughter or a divorced one."

I was sobbing. So was she. My chest was violently heaving up and down. Billu was darting his eyes between us, alert. With no answer, my mother simply left the room. My sister was in one corner, silently crying over the turmoil breaking up our family.

nineteen
shame

MY DECISION TORE my family apart. The elders were distraught. My husband was heartbroken. My actions led Sharaf's family to openly and blatantly criticize my parents to anyone willing to listen. But I decided to hold onto my self-respect for the first time in my life.

"Fine," my father-in-law said after a few days. "If this is what she wants, we can't force her to stay in this marriage. She'll get her divorce, but she has to continue sitting in sessions with the arbitrator, and she'll return the jewelry she received as mahr when the divorce is finalized."

I knew my father-in-law threatened to take away my jewelry to create an incentive for me to stay in the relationship, but he didn't understand that it was a small price to pay for my peace.

We mostly had these meetings over the phone.

Sharaf went from stubbornly silent to reiterating how much he was hurting due to my actions. He also kept saying, with pride, that he was the one in the relationship who wasn't running away.

"Son," the arbitrator said one day. "You need to take responsibility for your actions."

It made little difference. I was exhausted. My words had dried along with my tears. I could see, even with the constant repetition, that my husband didn't fathom the reality of our situation.

It led me to wonder—did he actually not understand my feelings, or did he simply refuse to acknowledge it because that would mean he would have to make amends for his actions, as the arbitrator blatantly pointed out?

A few of my relatives came to see me one evening. My two aunts and an uncle stared at me with pure disgust.

"How dare you, how dare you utter that filthy word, being a daughter of this family?" one of them screamed.

"You have brought unimaginable shame on our entire family name!"

"Our ancestors are crying in their graves."

I had no response, only wishing if only there was a way I could cut open my chest and show them the atrocious pain I was in, and all I had to endure that had brought me to this. Even then, I did not think they would understand.

They huffed and sat with my mother in our living room. My father barely got out of his room these days.

"How did this happen?" one of my aunts asked.

"What kind of woman takes these kinds of steps?"

"Do you have any idea what people are saying about her character, your family?"

My mother started wailing again. "We did everything right. We tried to teach them the best behavior, mannerisms, and morals. I don't know where we went wrong!"

"It is the modern education you provided," my uncle mused, his face hinting he was in deep thought. "The freedom you have given them."

"Agreed." Another aunt nodded. "Cut off access to television and internet right now. It's clearly brainwashing the daughters and doing more harm than good."

My mother spared no chance to taunt me about the fact that I was the one smitten with Sharaf—which is why my parents had to marry me off to him. Now I was blaming them to cover up my mistake. She would also mentioned how he treated me was considered normal for husbands in our society; in fact, given how some husbands of the earlier generation were—he was one of the better ones.

There were days when I wondered if all these were worth it—the pain I was going through, the shame I was bringing on my family. I felt despair rise to my chest every time I thought of how disappointed my father was with me, or the hate I had evoked in my mother's heart. Maybe Sharaf wasn't the issue here; I was simply overreacting. I couldn't help but feel it would be easier just to go back and give us another chance; after all, that's what he wanted, too.

My phone was filled with texts and calls from Sharaf.

"I will always love you."

"I think about you all the time."

"You can't give up on us, please."

Sometimes I replied to him, sometimes I didn't. But every time I thought of returning to his life, it made me sick to my stomach. I couldn't go back to that. Even the thought of him made me anxious.

I began to wonder if these were the only possible realities of my life now—live with shame or die with suffocation.

twenty
suffering

I SPENT my days in isolation.

I began living in my bedroom. I ate after all the other family members had finished their meals to avoid running into anyone. I kept to myself and took care of Billu. My only interaction with my family was when my sister slipped into our shared bed late at night, but even then, we barely made eye contact. I have always been close to my sister, but even she was afraid to come in contact with me in fear of our parents' reaction. I was an anomaly in the delusion of our picture-perfect family. An uncomfortable topic in our community.

The arbitrator tried to explain to my parents that my marriage had real concerns, which my husband would not address—yet I was still shunned from society. Sharaf, on the other hand, was the recipient of sympathy of not only his and my parents, but of our social circle as a whole.

One day, I received a call from my friend from the mosque.

"How's it going, Neela?"

The familiarity of her voice soothed the anguish in my heart. I once had friends from school and university. However, I rarely kept up with people outside of my family so the connections faded away over time. But when the individuals I considered to be my own couldn't stand the sight of me, I warmly welcomed this woman into my heart. I told her everything, starting from our first visit to the arbitrator to the aftermath of my asking for divorce.

"My family isn't even speaking to me," I said miserably. "They blame me for ruining everything."

"My love, we live in a broken society," she replied. "Your husband disrespected you, lied, and betrayed the trust of your marriage—but all people can focus on is that you're the one who's asking for a divorce. People expect women to endure even if it's beyond our capability and forgive even when it's unfair. They forget we're humans too, with feelings, indignance, and rights."

I let her words sink in. "My aunts and uncles think I'm brainwashed by the internet."

At this, she lets out a low chuckle. "The women of the previous generation are so used to bearing this pain they have convinced even themselves that this is the norm. They endured it, and so have their mothers and grandmothers, so when they see a woman finally standing up for herself, they don't understand what to make out of it."

Standing up for myself. This is the first time someone put it like this instead of perceiving my actions negatively. However, my heart was too burdened to share her optimism.

"A single day hasn't passed where I haven't second-guessed my decision," I confessed, my voice strained with emotions. "I sometimes don't know if I can actually hold onto my resolution till the end. At times, it feels like I'm making a grave mistake because that's what everyone keeps telling me."

She patiently listened to everything I had to say. Then she said, "Do you think going back to him will do either of you any good?"

I took a moment to ponder.

"No," I responded. "Every time I think of picking up that relationship, I can't even begin to tell you how my stomach recoils. Each of his apologies has been followed by blame thrown at me for being the source of the problem." My face twisted with resentment. "So tell me, how is that a real apology?" I sighed. "I can't bring myself to love him like I once did, not after everything that happened. The only way I can ever be with him again is if I kill my heart, stop myself from feeling things. The only future I see for us, together, is of two bitter people stuck in an unwanted marriage, raising a family of individuals who only loathe each other."

"Then you have your answer," she said. "Remember this the next time you feel pressured to go back to him. Divorce is not considered a sin by Islam—it is only believed so by our people. If you have done what you can and must now go through with divorce for the sake of your happiness, so be it. Our religion doesn't force you to endure disrespect and mistreatment; it encourages you to take action for your well-being. Hold onto your strength."

"How?" I asked helplessly.

"By remembering that the one Who created you has given you this right and, therefore, the strength to endure it. And when Allah gives you strength, nobody can take it away from you."

I swallowed, meekly nodding, feeling overwhelmed by emotions and information.

"Also, remember that you're not alone, even though that's how you feel right now," she said, kindness coating her voice. "If you believe it is the right decision for you, stick to it, even if it feels impossible at times."

I bid her goodbye and was about to hang up the phone. Then, I gathered my courage and asked the question that had been weighing down on my chest.

"Was it worth it?" I asked, voice merely a whisper. "Going through the divorce?"

I heard a sliver of that strength in her voice she talked about. "It was worth every ounce of suffering."

twenty-one
strength

MY SUFFERING CONTINUED.

The ugly words, pain, and anguish did not decrease by an inch.

But this time, I had something I did not have before—hope to achieve strength. For every filthy word hurled at me, for every sneer of disgust cast at me, I reminded myself that what I was doing was right for my sake.

Day after day, I prayed for strength. Strength to endure the pain and to pass this wave. I held onto my friend's words—words that simultaneously rooted hope and aroused curiosity within me. I was born and raised in a Muslim household and society. I was taught how to pray and read the Qur'an since I was a child, yet somehow, I felt like I was learning this religion for the first time when I talked to her. She and the arbitrator—they were different kinds of Muslims than the ones I was familiar with. They didn't blindly follow the cultural norms as religious values; they seemed to be truly in touch with their Faith more than anyone I knew.

I asked my friend for guidance; she provided me with links to videos on marital roles and laws. I learned that I didn't have to give up myself upon marriage; I was still my own person with dreams and desires. Though upon marriage my husband became my guardian, my parents still had rights over me. It was wrong of people to say my duties after marriage were only tied to my in-laws or that I was no longer my parents' daughter. Also, asking for a divorce didn't make me inauspicious or dirty. These were merely man-made superstitions.

I became more serious with my prayers and kept myself busy with increasing knowledge of my religion, not only in hopes of finding some peace in this time of madness but also to learn Islam correctly.

That elicited mocking jeers, too.

"She ruined the sanctity of a marriage and is now trying to act pious."

I reminded myself I was allowed to ask for divorce according to my religion and that this was well within my rights. My character couldn't be questioned for making this decision; people who said these things were back-biting and speaking without knowledge.

I often distracted myself by dreaming of a future

where I wasn't stuck in a society that deemed divorce to be worse than infidelity or more heinous than marital abuse. I imagined what it would be like to finally breathe and start to live again.

I reminded myself to be grateful for all I had. I was alive, healthy, and sheltered. I had parents who did not approve of the divorce but weren't forcing me to stay in the marriage either. For the first time in my life, I had Faith and clarity—and that was the most important of all.

I dreamed of an open meadow surrounded by green trees and wildflowers of every color. I imagined myself running through it, free and liberated. I imagined myself laughing, happy.

I did not forget to express gratitude for the hopes of a better future either. Because as long as I was alive, I had hope.

One day, I found my mother and sister arguing.

"This is a good proposal. The family is educated and wealthy. I don't understand why you're reluctant," my mother said hopelessly.

There was a deep frown between my sister's brows. She was mad, which was shocking because she was always a quiet and respectful girl.

"I'm still a college student," she said. "I'm always busy. I don't want to think about these things now."

"I'm not saying you have to get married tomorrow," my mother tried to reason. "Let's just see where it goes. Good proposals are hard to come by, and honestly, after all that happened," her lips formed a scowl, "I'm not sure if we have the luxury to reject any man."

My sister got to her feet in a whirl, emotions overtaking her. She started bawling.

"This is exactly why I don't want to get married!" she cried out. "I see what's happening to Neela. I know the things she has suffered. I'm witnessing how you all are treating her for it." Her hands trembled. "When I'm stuck in a miserable marriage with an abusive scoundrel, I think you'd all just let me die with my pain because that is less shameful than a divorce in this household!"

She stormed off, and my mother stared at her figure, dumbfounded.

I sat on my sister's bed later that evening. Her anger had cooled, her tears had stopped, and she was staring at the wall opposite her room with an empty look in her eyes.

"Not every man is terrible, not every marriage ends with a heartbreak," I told her with a sigh. "It is our Fate that we had to come across one."

"I have seen enough to know that this scenario is more common than its happier counterpart," she said without turning to me, voice cold and rigid.

"But it could also workout. You could find a man who is good for you and respects you. Aren't you curious to find out what it would be like to be happily married and in love?" I asked, voicing a dream I wasn't sure would reach me again. "Sometimes in life we have to take risks in hopes of a better future."

She sat up in one swift movement, eyes wet with tears and pain again. "You can't promise me a better future. No one can," she said, indignant.

"You're right." I let out a sigh. "Nothing in life is guaranteed. But recently, I learned a thing or two about Faith," I said after a moment of thought. "Before a big exam, we study with all our might with the hope that our efforts will lead to good grades, even though there is no certainty that we'll achieve our desired result, right?"

Her eyes searched mine, curiosity peaking in them.

"We do that because we have this in-built Faith that allows us to have hope. We have a Lord who loves us and will take care of us if we pray to Him, rely upon Him, and show with our actions that we're deserving of success." As my sister opened her mouth to refute I added, "A happy ending is still not guaranteed, I know, but if you can hold onto hope before your exams why can't do that for every other decision of your life? I choose to have Faith in that Lord and move forward in life with the hope of a good ending, and I ask you to do the same. This time around, we will be more cautious before agreeing on a proposal," I continued. "We'll do our due diligence with Faith in our hearts. I think our parents will agree to avoid another situation similar to mine."

"It's too difficult. What if he turns out worse than Sh-Sharaf?" she fumbled, her eyes suddenly lost and desperate. "What will I do then?"

"Then you'll leave him," I said simply.

She looked up, disbelief in her gaze. "After everything you've been through, do you still think it's something I'll be able to survive?"

"I do," I said. "Because now you have a sister who has already been through it. And no matter what, despite how your heart aches, you'll know that you'll have my full support through it all."

twenty-two
healing

MY FRIEND CALLED ME AGAIN. We talked for hours as if I had known her for years, filling each other in about the other's lives.

"Neela, have you ever considered getting a job?" she suddenly asked.

I was taken by surprise. "A job?" I repeated.

"Yes, a job," she affirmed enthusiastically. "You have a good education. It shouldn't be hard for you to find one. It's not mandatory for a woman to work, but I think this could be good for you as it'll give you a break from everything."

The thought didn't even occur to me. Before marriage, my family expected me to look for jobs or pursue a higher degree after graduation. Though my parents were conservative in other ways, they believed in educating their daughters and encouraged them to pursue careers. However, since Sharaf didn't allow me to spend too much out of the house, let alone get a job or a degree, those plans were put to rest.

"I wouldn't even know where to begin," I told her with a shrug.

"My husband and I are starting a school. It's still new, but it shows potential," she said with a chuckle. "We're looking for new teachers for a variety of subjects. Since you are in iddah, you can start with the after-school online courses. Do you think you'd be interested in that?"

I chewed my bottom lip, thinking. I had three months of iddah—the waiting period for a woman who divorces in case she is pregnant—to complete the divorce. But being in the house was pins and needles. I knew women weren't obligated to work, but it was permitted in our religion. I thought back to how she said it would provide an escape.

"Okay," I replied, my tone still hesitant.

"Great!" she exclaimed. "We can sit down for a meeting tomorrow morning. I'll send you the link by tonight. We can discuss things over and see if we can find something for you that benefits both parties."

I was nervous all night. And then all morning. But it all melted away when I sat across from the laptop screen and saw my friend. She joined the meeting with her husband, and he was just as nice as her. They made me feel like I had absolutely nothing to worry about.

The meeting went successfully, and by the end of it, they both told me they liked me and wanted me to start with an after-school Math course for Standard II students.

Despite my hesitations, I agreed.

My parents were already so upset with me over everything that they had given up on me completely by this point, so they had little to no reaction over this news. My sister was excited for me. To show support, she woke up early along with me on my first day of work to show support and wish me the best.

The first couple of weeks were rocky. Waking up early, maintaining a schedule, maintaining professionalism—these things didn't come easily to me. But I was a fast learner, and I was hard working.

My friend was right; it became a channel for me to forget the instability of my house and mind. Soon, I started finding joy in the work I did. As I was buried with work, it let me forget the turmoil in my mind, even if briefly. I was finally starting to feel like myself, little by little.

The owners of the school—my friend and her husband—the coordinator of the junior section, and our team's supervisor sometimes held group meetings online to have all the teachers familiarize themselves with each other. I kept mostly to myself. The rest of the employees, including our coordinator and supervisor, were women. They were also older and more experienced, but none with a past as dark as mine. I only engaged with them regarding work and the cute but rascal students and let minimum distractions bother my mind.

Soon, a few of my colleagues started chatting with me. If there's one thing I learned, it's that teachers love to chat. We started sharing ideas and personal information. Before I knew it, they called me even beyond school hours.

Once, while having a casual chat with one of the ladies, I slipped that I was in the middle of a divorce. I regretted it instantly. I expected her to sneer at me, say hurtful words like everyone else.

But my work-friend took it in stride, as if these things happen and aren't a stain on one's character.

She even said, "It takes guts to do what you did, Neela."

twenty-three
peace

AS DAYS PASSED, things in my house grew even more restless. The waiting period was drawing to an end, which meant the final formalities of the procedure needed to be discussed.

I could feel the pressure. My parents now refused to even look at me most days, let alone speak to me. Anxiety and dread became a regular part of my daily life, even more so than before. I spent most of my time locked in my room, which I shared with my sister and Billu, or I kept myself busy with work.

A month had passed since I started my new job, and soon, I received my first salary. My father earned a sufficient amount, and he never failed to take care of our needs. I wanted to do something nice for my parents in return, also hoping it would melt the ice between us. So, I spent the majority of the money to buy groceries for my family, with the help of my sister.

My father was furious. "The day I accept money from you is the day I spit on my ancestors' graves."

I was hurt, but I also knew that whether he accepted my gift or not wasn't my business. I was doing what I could for my parents to the best of my ability. And that was enough for me.

I was finishing online classes when I was informed Sharaf was here. I stepped into the room to find him waiting for me.

My heart skipped a beat in an uncomfortable way.

He looked different, almost nothing like the man I once loved. His hair was disheveled, his beard wasn't trimmed, and there were bags under his eyes from all the sleepless nights. I was taken back by surprise—Sharaf had always been proper and groomed. The man in front of me looked broken, and not just for his appearance.

His rich brown eyes met mine, and a soft breath left his lips.

"Neela," he called.

My name sounded toxic coming from his mouth.

He was watching me desperately, drinking in my appearance. "You haven't been replying to my calls or texts."

I walked forward and took a seat somewhere beside him without a word.

"Your mother says you've started working," he stated, the disapproval clear in his eyes.

"Yes," I replied, with a glimmer of pride in mine for overcoming all I did. His opinion of me no longer mattered to me.

There was a heavy pause between us.

"I miss you," he said, voice getting thick with emotions,

"No," I said softly. "You only miss the way I made you feel."

And the control you had over me.

He pursed his lips. "I've been thinking about you a lot." He swallowed. "Us, the moments we spent and the future we always dreamed of together. How could you let it all go, Neela?" His eyes were starting to water; I was afraid he would start sobbing again. "Don't you ever think about it?"

"No," I responded honestly.

My answer hurt him deeply. He looked down, unable to look into my eyes anymore without falling apart.

"I—I never realized how much I loved you until I lost you. I didn't think my heart would hurt half as much as it is now," he confessed.

"That fact that you didn't think you'd be upset if your wife left you should tell you why I took the decision," I said.

"But I get it now," he insisted. "I miss you, baby," he said, that desperate look in his eyes searching for me again. "I want you back. I'm sorry. Let's forget all this." He reached out, placing a gentle hand on my knee. "Don't punish me like this for one stupid mistake. Don't throw away our marriage over something so silly," he pleaded.

A wry smile appeared on my lips. "You say you're sorry, yet you've only been talking about your needs and wants since the moment I arrived. If you wanted our marriage to work, shouldn't you be considering my feelings? Instead, you are belittling your mistreatment of me, as always."

He moved closer to me, that hand still on my knee. "How can I make it better? What can I do that will make you forget all about it? I know we can still make it work."

I let out a sigh. "No, we can't." I gently lifted the hand on my leg and removed it. "Please never touch me without my permission again."

Disbelief crossed his features. His eyes kept searching mine as if still looking for me.

"You've changed," he stated, looking slightly offended.

"I have," I said.

I got up to my feet, and I stared at him for a moment. All I saw was a manipulative man who refused to think beyond his selfish needs, made broken by my choice to be free from them.

"Don't leave, Neela." His voice cracked. "I still love you. I always will. We can be happy again."

I was already at the door, and I unlocked it. I dared to look back, glancing at him over my shoulder. He was crying now. I felt nothing but pity in my heart.

"Have a nice life, Sharaf," I said, a part of me genuinely wishing he would find peace in his heart someday.

I stepped out of the door and went up to the balcony. Letting out a deep breath, lightening the heaviness of my heart. I stayed there while I waited for him to leave, the free breeze battering against my face.

twenty-four
breathe

MY IDDAH WAS COMPLETE. The divorce was finalized.

It was a new day. A new morning. The sun was shining brightly. The sky was a clear blue. A wind blew past. I wondered if nature could feel the peace in my heart, too.

I was smiling. I was laughing. My eyes found my colleagues at the other end of the field. There was an annual school function going on, there were joyful squeals of kids all around.

"Neela!" one of my colleagues called. "This man is selling these scarves; come check it out with us."

I was being dragged by the hand before I could respond.

"Blue!" one of my work friends cried, picking up a silk blue scarf. She wrapped it around my arms. "Blue, like you always wear."

I wrinkled my nose. "I don't want blue. I want..." My eyes searched the colorful clothes hanging from the hooks. "That one!" I pointed at a bright green scarf. "I want green."

"Like moss?" she quipped.

"No, like the leaves dancing in the wind," I responded.

She smiled at me fondly, shaking her head at my playful eyes.

I wrapped the green scarf around my shoulders with satisfaction. I disliked blue even as a child, the color never suited me. And nobody could force me to wear it any longer.

My eyes found my sister in the sea of crowds, acting as a volunteer for the event. She excitedly waved at me, and I waved back with just as enthusiasm.

"C'mon!" one of my friends held my hand, veering my attention once more, leading me in another direction.

I went with her, the scarf blowing behind me with the wind, with a smile on my face.

I was learning to breathe again.

epilogue

FOR YEARS AFTER, very little changed in others' treatment of me. My parents continued to refuse to accept my divorce, society still sneered at me, and I lived like an unwanted guest in my own house.

Pain is a strange thing. We spend our lives trying to avoid it. When we're in it, we can't wait to part from it. But only after it has passed do we realize that pain is a necessary part of life that teaches us the capacity of our own strength.

Life as a divorced woman has given me immense pain—but within that pain, I found my strength, my identity, and ultimately, my freedom.

During those years I learned to love my Faith, stand up for myself, and found friends who saw me beyond the banner of divorce—as a person with hopes and dreams.

People's treatment of me remained unchanged, but how I felt about it did.

While I was working in the teacher's room one afternoon, a school counselor was hanging out with us. I mostly kept my past where it belonged—in the past. But in the few instances when I had difficulty seeing beyond the dark clouds, I sought out this lady. Talking to her always soothed my heart, like hearing the lullaby of crashing waves.

Hearing my tales, she once told me, "Neela, the way you talk about him, it seems to me like he was emotionally abusive."

This was the first time I heard that term, and my stomach churned uncomfortably. He wasn't a good husband, but he was still someone I once loved and considered family at some point in life. Seeing him in that light and attaching that term to my broken marriage was a bitter pill to swallow. However, I owed it to myself to see and accept the truth.

When my sister finally got married, I ensured we did our due diligence before she agreed to the proposal. She had a few chaperoned meetings with him. They asked each other questions about Faith and their future plans while she tried to look for the qualities of a caring husband. We also asked around in the community to get an understanding of the man's reputation. We can never be sure that all our efforts and prayers will lead to a happy marriage, but I was glad that my sister chose him because she believed they were compatible—not because she fell for his charms or due to pressure from society.

As I watched the new couple laugh together, I was reminded of the yearning my younger self once felt; to find love, have children and build my own family. The yearning was still in me, but it had been overshadowed by trauma and the aftermath of the divorce all this time.

I felt myself opening up to the idea of marrying again; maybe I would be blessed to find someone I could stay in love with, and vice versa. We could start a family; maybe I would quit my job and focus on our children, or I would continue working—whichever he and I decide was best suited for our family. I could see myself building a life with him—a life where the foundations were love, Faith, and respect.

acknowledgments

بِسْمِ اللهِ الرَّحْمٰنِ الرَّحِيْمِ

I begin with the name of the One who created me and thus granted me the ability to see, feel, and write. It is Allah Who bestowed me with every ounce of knowledge I acquire, sowed the seed of this story in my heart, and allowed it to flow through my fingertips. I'm overjoyed that I was chosen to share this story with the world, and I hope I have done it justice. Every goodness in this book is from Him, and every wrong is from me.

I would not have been able to publish this book without the help of my editor and publisher Samiha from the Shaherazad Shelves. Thank you for recognizing the potential of this book even from its earliest draft. It is your vision that allowed it to come as far as it did.

I express my deepest gratitude towards the woman who raised me, taught me how to read and write—my mother. Every one of my successes is a result of your unsung sacrifices. I would also like to extend my thanks and appreciation to Hiba Fathima, a second-year student of B.Sc Psychology, for helping me with the abuse in the story and for giving me clarity about the abuser and the victim's behaviors wherever needed. A special thanks to the sweet individual (who chose to remain anonymous) for helping me ensure this story follows proper Islamic guidelines.

Last but not least, I thank every single one of my friends who read this book and provided me with feedback—Saroosh, Sharifah, Amu, and Sumaiya. Some of you read the earliest draft of the book and still liked it with all its rough edges. It is with your encouraging words that I move forward.

about the author

K. Mostafa is a Bangladeshi author and began her writing journey as an avid reader. After many years, she started sharing her written work on Wattpad as a teenager to spend her free time. Her book *Sapphire* has since garnered over 100k reads and was featured as a Wattpad Short Story.

While writing started as a hobby for K. Mostafa, it has now become a passion. Born and raised in a chaotic desi family, her favorite topics to explore as an author are complicated family ties and cultural traditions knee-deep in religious misconceptions.

When she is not writing, K. Mostafa enjoys slow mornings, cooking for her family, and taking care of her plants. She's an extreme introvert who's married to the most extroverted man. Visit her online on Instagram (@makekatmatter) or Wattpad (https://www.wattpad.com/user/makeitmatter).

www.ingramcontent.com/pod-product-compliance
Lightning Source LLC
Chambersburg PA
CBHW010356310726
48979CB00006B/1057

* 9 7 8 1 9 6 0 3 2 3 3 2 3 *